MY
NEW BOY

As a part of the HBJ TREASURY OF LITERATURE, 1993 Edition, this edition is published by special arrangement with Random House, Inc.

Grateful acknowledgment is made to Random House, Inc. for permission to reprint *My New Boy* by Joan Phillips, illustrated by Lynn Munsinger. Text copyright © 1986 by Joan Phillips; illustrations copyright © 1986 by Lynn Munsinger.

Printed in the United States of America

ISBN 0-15-300313-8

MY NEW BOY

by Joan Phillips

illustrated by Lynn Munsinger

HBJ Harcourt Brace Jovanovich, Inc.
Orlando Austin San Diego Chicago Dallas New York

I am a little black puppy.

I live in a pet store.

Soon I will have

a kid of my own.

Many kids come.

This one pulls my tail.

This one kisses too much.

They are not for me.

Here is another kid.

He says hello.

He pats my head.

Woof! Woof!

This is the boy for me!

My new boy takes me home.

I start taking care
of my boy right away.

I help him eat dinner.

I keep him clean.

I teach him to play
tug of war.

I teach him to throw
a ball to me.

I show my boy tricks.

I sit up.

I roll over.

I teach my boy
to give me a bone
every time I do a trick.

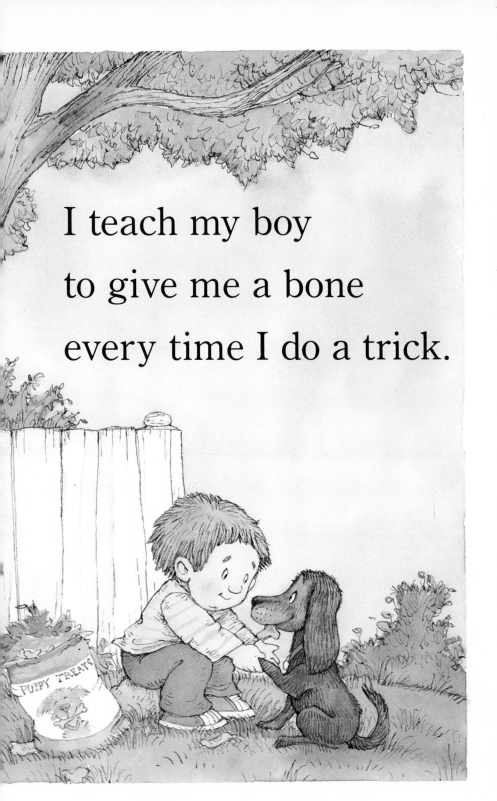

My boy is not good
at everything.

He can not dig very fast.

He can not scratch his ears
with his foot.

He can not hide
under the bed.

My boy can not run
as fast as I can.

I run and run.

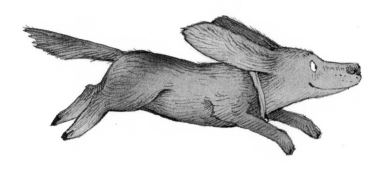

Oh, no!

I do not see my boy.

Is he lost?

I look behind a tree.

I look on the rocks.
I do not see my boy.

Is he on the swing?
No.

Is he on the slide?

No.

I do not see
my boy anywhere.

Now I see my boy.

He sees me too.

He is happy

I found him.

We go home.

Woof! Woof! Woof!

I tell my boy

he must not

get lost again.

My boy is lucky
to have a smart puppy
like me!